scamper

Brain

S0-AAD-413

IGOR KING PRESENTS

The Official 51st Annual Evil Science Fair

PROGRAM

BROUGHT TO YOU BY
ELIZA ELLIOT

*With a special page designed
by scamper and Brain!*

NEW YORK LONDON TORONTO SYDNEY MALARIA

Based on the screenplay by Chris McKenna

SIMON SPOTLIGHT

An imprint of Simon & Schuster Children's Publishing Division
1230 Avenue of the Americas, New York, New York 10020

Manufactured in the United States of America
First Edition
2 4 6 8 10 9 7 5 3 1
ISBN-13: 978-1-4169-5448-4
ISBN-10: 1-4169-5448-1

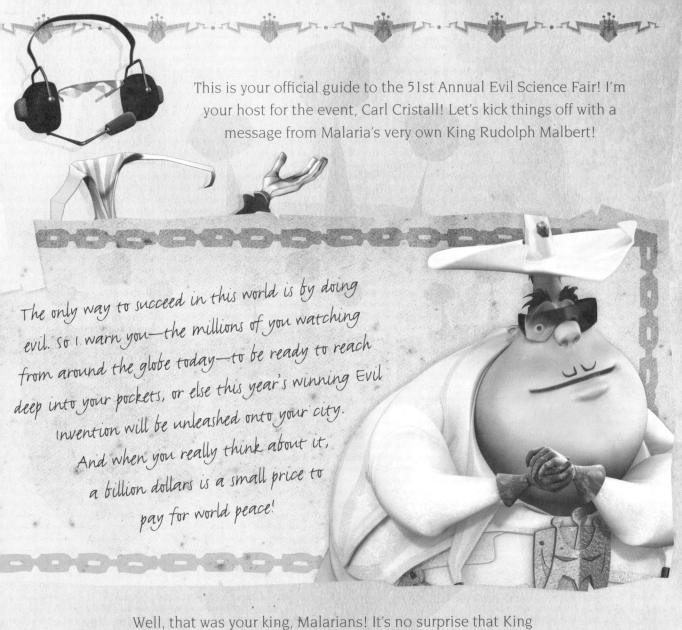

This is your official guide to the 51st Annual Evil Science Fair! I'm your host for the event, Carl Cristall! Let's kick things off with a message from Malaria's very own King Rudolph Malbert!

The only way to succeed in this world is by doing evil. So I warn you—the millions of you watching from around the globe today—to be ready to reach deep into your pockets, or else this year's winning Evil invention will be unleashed onto your city. And when you really think about it, a billion dollars is a small price to pay for world peace!

Well, that was your king, Malarians! It's no surprise that King Malbert has just been named *World* magazine's richest man in the galaxy! And now, without further ado, let's get evil!

STATS

Contests entered: 17
Contests won: 17 (in a row!)
Igors recycled: 28
Graduated from M.I.E.T.*   GPA: 2.5
*(Malaria's Institute of Evil Technology)

DR. FREDERICK SCHADENFREUDE

RIGHT-HAND GAL

Often seen arguing with Schadenfreude, devoted
girlfriend Jaclyn has been by Schadenfreude's side
since his first Evil Science Fair win!

EVIL BACKGROUND

It's a little-known fact that Dr. Schadenfreude comes from a long line of pickle-makers.
His great-grandfather Alfred Poekelmacher was the original owner of Malaria's Famous
Pickle Factory—home of the famous pickled chili peppers. Schadenfreude worked in the
family factory until he fell into a tub of brine, turning his attitude forever salty.
Soon after, Schadenfreude sold the factory and dedicated his life to evil.

EVIL ENTRY

It's a mystery! (Just like his low G.P.A. . . .) In classic Schadenfreude style, he never reveals his Evil Invention before the contest begins, for fear that someone may steal it. Clearly, this undefeated genius has a reason to be paranoid!

ONE-ON-ONE

Q: What were you like when you were young?

A: Evil, of course! In elementary school I was voted "most likely to steal your lunch money"!

OVERHEARD SAYING

"I will not be beaten down by a hunchbacked, pot-bellied, bulgy-eyed runt!"

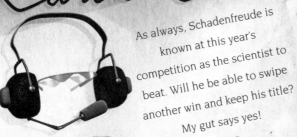

Carl's Call

As always, Schadenfreude is known at this year's competition as the scientist to beat. Will he be able to swipe another win and keep his title? My gut says yes!

DID YOU KNOW?

• The origin of Schadenfreude's name is quite an interesting one! Here's the breakdown: Schaden = damage or harm; Freude = joy; Definition = one who delights in another's misfortune.

• He wrote an advice book for children called *How to Make Your Parents Vanish!*

STATS

Contests entered: 31

Contests won: 2

Igors recycled: 19

Graduated from M.I.E.T.*   GPA: 3.5

*(Malaria's Institute of Evil Technology)

DR. HERMAN GLICKENSTEIN

RIGHT-HAND GAL

Dr. Glickenstein received his affectionate nickname, "Poopschoen," from his longtime girlfriend, Heidi.

EVIL BACKGROUND

Young Glickenstein was the unfortunate brunt of many bullies' pranks, forcing Mother Glickenstein to scold anyone who taunted him. Poor young Glicky soon earned the reputation of a mama's boy. When Glickenstein grew up, he vowed to create the ultimate Evil Invention—not only as a payback to the bullies of his past, but to make Mummy proud. Glickenstein is finally unveiling his evil rocket ship—which he has affectionately named after his mother, Gladys.

EVIL ENTRY
EVIL ROCKET SHIP

As Glickenstein told us, "The rocket was born to stream through the world, unleashing pain and misery!"

ONE-ON-ONE

Q: Are you afraid this year's entry might be a failure?

A: You sound like my mummy—you old cow!

OVERHEARD SAYING

"Think! Igors don't think!"

Carl's Call

Glickenstein is known for having a bad track record. Will this year's rocket ship be able to take flight and blast its way into first place? I guess we'll have to wait to find out!

DID YOU KNOW?

- He gives his Igor five minutes a week to take care of personal business. This generous act makes him a favorite among Malaria's Igors.
- He dislikes kittens.
- He has a robotic right hand.
- Mummy Glickenstein cooks Glicky dinner every Tuesday, Thursday, and Sunday.

STATS

Contests entered: 9
Contests won: 0
Igors recycled: 14
Graduated from M.I.E.T.*   GPA: 3.1
*(Malaria's Institute of Evil Technology)

DR. DIETER KINDERMANN

EVIL BACKGROUND

The youngest of twenty-two children, Dr. Kindermann always enjoyed being the baby of the family. As he grew older, Kindermann became jealous of younger generations. In his attempts to stay young, he began experimenting with age-altering potions. Eventually, Kindermann headed to Malaria to perfect his "youth formula" and destroy any youngsters who dared cross his path.

EVIL ENTRY
EVIL TEDDY BEAR

This marionette teddy bear challenges victims with martial arts.

ONE-ON-ONE

Q: I see that your newest anti-aging formula shrank your head. Have you figured out a way to reverse this side effect?

A: You're mean! I want my mummy!

Carl's Call

Kindermann is still a less-experienced competitor, and I don't think he's quite mature enough to have what it takes to win. My prediction: This invention will be full of fluff! Let's just say that I don't think this teddy is a black belt.

DID YOU KNOW?

- His favorite drink is milk.
- He always travels with his trademark blue bunny.
- He enjoys being burped after a hearty meal.
- His favorite book in school was Mother Goose's Nursery Rhymes.

STATS

Contests entered: 22
Contests won: 4
Igors recycled: 39
Graduated from M.I.E.T.*   GPA: 3.7
*(Malaria's Institute of Evil Technology)

DR. FRITZ HERTZSCHLAG

HERTZSCHLAG'S IGOR

EVIL BACKGROUND

Dr. Hertzschlag used to be known as *Chef* Hertzschlag! In fact, he owned one of the most famous restaurants in the world. People would travel for miles for just a small bite of one of his rich and decadent dishes. Then, one unfortunate night, some spoiled meat was served to a testy taster. The diner wrote a review so distasteful that Hertzschlag had to close his prized restaurant forever! The very next day, Herztschlag moved to Malaria. . . .

EVIL ENTRY

BLOB

This mysterious blob suffocates victims
and eats them.

ONE-ON-ONE

Q: Everyone wants to know: How many chins do you have?
A: I've never been sure. . . . I lost count when I was thirteen!

Carl's Call

Will Hertzschlag's entry receive rave reviews?
I think that this blob may have more bounce
than we bargained for. On my word, if this
four-star invention doesn't get into the
semifinals, I'll eat my (invisible) foot!

DID YOU KNOW?

- He hosts Malaria's horror-movie marathon.
- He loves Malaria's all-you-can-eat buffet.
- His favorite kinds of pie are apple, cherry, lemon, lime, peach, pecan, pumpkin mincemeat, strawberry, strawberry-rhubarb, blueberry, blackberry, raspberry, mixed berry, chocolate, chocolate-peanut butter, coconut . . .

PHOTO DEEP-SIXED

STATS

Contests entered: 11

Contests won: 1

Igors recycled: 26

Graduated from M.I.E.T.*

GPA: 3.2

*(Malaria's Institute of Evil Technology)

EVIL BACKGROUND

Growing up by the seaside, Dr. Tintenfisch spent hours exploring the depths of the ocean. During one journey, Tintenfisch fell in love with a beautiful mermaid. But the beauty rejected Tintenfisch, and he was left tormented. Years passed, and Tintenfisch grew angry about his failed romance. He studied sea creatures that sting and strangle their prey (much like the sting he felt in his heart), and these became the inspiration for his latest Evil Invention.

ONE-ON-ONE

Q: Did you always see yourself as an Evil Scientist? Or did you want to be something different when you were a kid?

A: I wanted to help salmon swim upriver!

DID YOU KNOW?

- He collects seashells.
- He has a metal lung.

EVIL ENTRY

OCTOPUS

This squasher of love wraps people in its tentacles and strangles them.

Carl's Call

After last year's display, I can only hope that Tintenfisch's invention this year isn't all washed up. He'll have to make a pretty impressive comeback for everyone to forget about the dead fish he presented last year—what a rotten way to go!

DR. HANS GROANER

DR. ABDUCTED PRIOR TO TAKING PHOTO

STATS

Contests entered: 15

Contests won: 3

Igors recycled: 22

Graduated from M.I.E.T.*

(Malaria's Institute of Evil Technology)

GPA: 3.73

EVIL BACKGROUND

When Groaner was a boy, he snapped photos of a UFO through his telescope, and the photos became famous. Dr. Groaner went on to become one of the world's most acclaimed astronomers. Years later, it leaked that Groaner's famous photographs were fake. Groaner was a laughingstock! So he quickly moved to Malaria to build a UFO that no one would mistake for a fake.

DID YOU KNOW?

He's president of UFOs 'R' Us. His favorite snack is the Mars Bar.

ONE-ON-ONE

Q: Do you plan to tie the knot with your longtime girlfriend anytime soon?

A: Sure, I'll marry Hanna when life is discovered on Pluto.

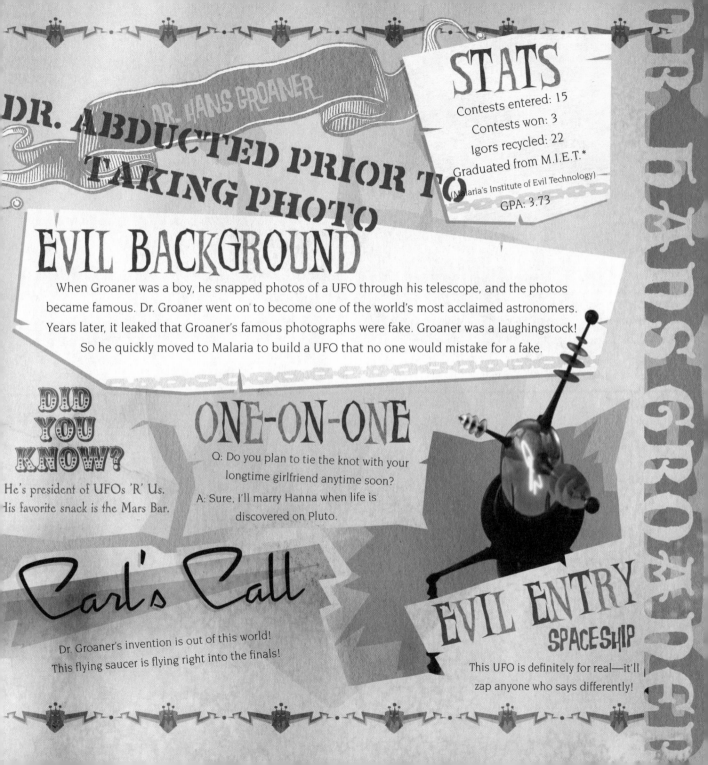

Carl's Call

Dr. Groaner's invention is out of this world! This flying saucer is flying right into the finals!

EVIL ENTRY
SPACESHIP

This UFO is definitely for real—it'll zap anyone who says differently!

DR. SONYA HOLZWURM

STATS

Contests entered: 14
Contests won: 2
Igors recycled: 59 (and counting!)
Graduated from M.I.E.T.*   GPA: 3.57
*(Malaria's Institute of Evil Technology)

HOLZWURM'S IGOR

EVIL BACKGROUND

Born into a rich family, Dr. Holzwurm had all the luxuries a girl could ever want. One day, while on a shopping spree, Holzwurm got caught in the mix of local Earth Day parade marchers! The parade opened her eyes to a more environmentally-friendly way of life. Holzwurm gave up her materialistic ways and dedicated her life to protecting the environment—and attacking anyone who harms it!

EVIL ENTRY

PLANT MONSTER

This monster paralyzes victims with venomous gas. (Environmentally safe, of course!)

ONE-ON-ONE

Q: What was your inspiration for this year's invention?

A: The Venus fly trap, of course!

Carl's Call

Holzwurm has really outdone herself this year! This Plant Monster has a real chance to bloom in the competition. Let me put it this way: The Plant's victims should be scared stiff—literally!

DID YOU KNOW?

- She uses all-natural ingredients in her evil formulas.
- She is the only vegetarian scientist in this year's competition.
- She founded Malaria's Igor Recycling Day.

designed by Brain and scamper

scamper,
the Great!

Stats

Contents entered: 0
Contests won: 0
~~Igors recycled: 0~~

Hunches: 1

Brian
Brain
(The brains
of the group)

BRAIN

Evil
Background

Like all Igors, this poor hunchback was unjustly thrown
into a life of pulling switches and cleaning test tubes.
But this Igor was determined not to be just another
nobody. A last-minute contestant in this year's
competition, Igor has seized his opportunity to submit his
own Evil invention, which, as rumor has it, just happens
to be LIFE! Unfortunately, I have heard rumblings that
this brilliant invention—the great actress Eva—was born
without an evil bone in her mismatched body.

Evil Entry
(and Right-hand Gal)
Eva
• Igor is also Eva's talent manager.

One-on-One

Q: Igor, is it true that you are entering this year's competition illegally?

A: I, uh, what? Where's Eva? I have to find Eva!

Overheard Saying

"Everyone has an evil bone in their body, but we choose whether or not to use it."

Carl's Call

Well, there you have it, folks—the rumors are true. And it seems like this little Igor who could has not only created an actress named Eva, but now he's lost her! As for his chances tonight, they were looking promising at first, but without proof of life, this Igor's on his way to the recycling bin!

Did You Know?

• He once had a secret crush on Dr. Glickenstein's girlfriend, Heidi.
• His favorite fashion accessory is a beret.
• He likes dogs and dislikes the cha-cha.
• He directs local community plays for blind orphans.

...or is green.

STATS

Contests entered: 12
Contests won: 2
Igors recycled: 39
Graduated from M.I.E.T.*   GPA: 3.64
*(Malaria's Institute of Evil Technology)

DR. MARKUS NIEMAND

NIEMAND AND HIS IGOR

EVIL BACKGROUND

Niemand grew up in a house full of animals—literally! His parents were veterinarians who studied the wildlife of a lush and beautiful rainforest. However, as he grew older, Niemand became bored with the native animals of his homeland—such as elephants, zebras, hyenas, and snakes—and longed to discover more exotic wildlife. So he came to Malaria to create a unique creature, something the world has never seen before!

EVIL ENTRY
GRIFFIN

This exotic invention shoots laser beams out of its eyes!

ONE-ON-ONE

Q: What is the most evil animal you've discovered?
A: My pet Chihuahua. Of course, I've *trained* him to be evil!

Carl's Call

This beast looks like it is too wild to be tamed! I can't wait to see how the competition reacts to the unleashing of this animal!

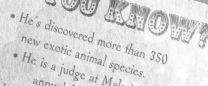

DID YOU KNOW?

- He's discovered more than 350 new exotic animal species.
- He is a judge at Malaria's annual dog show.
- His shoe size is an enormous twenty-two.

DR. MAXIMILLIAN BAZILLUS

DID NOT WANT TO BE BUGGED FOR PHOTO

STATS

Contests entered: 4

Contests won: 2

Igors recycled: 14

Graduated from M.I.E.T.*

GPA: 3.3

*(Malaria's Institute of Evil Technology)

EVIL BACKGROUND

Bazillus's fascination with insects began with his first ant farm, a science fair entry that earned him first place. He began studying all creepy-crawlers—worms, cockroaches, and spiders. The only thing that bothered Bazillus about his beloved bugs was that they were so small! He decided to give insects the respect they deserve, and set out to create the biggest bug the world had ever seen.

ONE-ON-ONE

Q: Have any of your caterpillars ever changed into butterflies?

A: BUZZ OFF!

DID YOU KNOW?

• He's the founder of Malaria's Horrifying Horticultural Society.

EVIL ENTRY

KILLER CATERPILLAR

This killer bug camouflages itself, sneaks up on its victim, and then injects toxins into the prey.

Carl's Call

Bazillus's Killer Caterpillar might not be the frontrunner in the fair, but it could have the ability to annoy its fellow competitors out of the first few rounds. We may not be able to get rid of this irritating invention.

PHOTO LOST IN AN ALTERNATE DIMENSION

DR. LEO NACTMAHR

DR. LEO NACTMAHR

STATS

Contests entered: 14

Contests won: 0

Igors recycled: 22

Graduated from M.I.E.T.*

GPA: 3.8

*(Malaria Institute of Evil Technology)

EVIL BACKGROUND

Leo Nactmahr grew up in the sun-drenched countryside with his family, where his brothers and sisters enjoyed playing outdoors and frolicking among the flowers. But, born allergic to the rays of the sun, poor Nactmahr was a prisoner in his own house. Nactmahr entered M.I.E.T. to get revenge on everyone with a sunny disposition.

DID YOU KNOW?

He worked the night shift a local diner to put himself through school.

ONE-ON-ONE

Q: What is your favorite day of the year?

A: The first day of winter. It is also known as the longest night of the year!

Carl's Call

Nactmahr's Black Hole is in a galaxy of its own! It's an interesting entry, but we'll have to wait and see if it has the power to suck in the competition.

EVIL ENTRY
BLACK HOLE

This invention is the opposite of sun, sucking people into blackness so they are lost forever.

DR. FRANZ BLITZKRIEG

BLITZKRIEG'S IGOR

EVIL BACKGROUND

Dr. Blitzkrieg is a distant relative of the genius Albert Einstein. As a kid he spent his days and nights tinkering with metals and inventing small gadgets. Because Blitzkrieg inherited the family knack for science, his parents enrolled him in the elite School of Science. But Blitzkrieg, always jealous of his great-great-uncle Einstein's celebrity, sought his own fame and transferred to M.I.E.T.—and graduated with honors.

EVIL ENTRY

ELECTRIC ORB

This ball of genius shoots electricity at its victims.

ONE-ON-ONE

Q: What is your favorite kind of food?

A: Anything FRIED!

Carl's Call

Things are not looking so bright for Blitzkrieg this year. The Electric Orb is likely to get zapped by the competition. In my opinion Blitzkrieg is burned out.

DID YOU KNOW?

- He's the tallest scientist in this year's fair.
- He has been struck by lightning nineteen times.
- He collects light bulbs.
- He's a member of the Evil Electromagnetism Enthusiasts Club.